Sneaky Sheep

by

Chris Monroe

CAROLRHODA BOOKS MINNEAPOLIS · NEW YORK

TO LAURIE AND MEG,
TWO SNEAKY SISTERS.
—C.M.

CAROLRHODA BOOKS
A DIVISION OF LERNER PUBLISHING GROUP, INC.
241 FIRST AVENUE NORTH
MINNEAPOLIS, MN 55401 U.S.A.

WEBSITE ADDRESS: WWW.LERNERBOOKS.COM

LIBRARY OF CONGRESS CATALOGING-IN-PUBLICATION DATA

MONROE, CHRIS.
   SNEAKY SHEEP / BY CHRIS MONROE ; ILLUSTRATED BY CHRIS MONROE.
      P.   CM.
   SUMMARY: BLOSSOM AND ROCKY, TWO SNEAKY AND NOT VERY BRIGHT SHEEP,
KEEP TRYING TO GET AWAY FROM THE REST OF THE FLOCK, IN SPITE OF THE
DANGERS THEY ENCOUNTER.
   ISBN: 978-0-7613-5615-8 (LIB. BDG. : ALK. PAPER)
   [1. SHEEP—FICTION. 2. BEHAVIOR—FICTION.] I. TITLE.
PZ7.M76OSN 2010
[E]—DC22   2009040852

MANUFACTURED IN THE UNITED STATES OF AMERICA
1 – DP – 7/15/10

Rocky and Blossom
lived in a meadow on
the mountain.

THEY LIVED WITH 147 OTHER
SHEEP AND A SHEEP DOG
NAMED MURPHY.

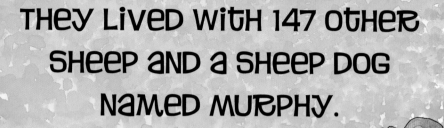

BAA-

MURPHY WATCHED OVER THE SHEEP. HE MADE
SURE THEY ALL STAYED IN THE MEADOW.

BUT BLOSSOM AND ROCKY DID NOT WANT
TO STAY IN THE MEADOW.

The Mountain

Snowy Peak

The High Meadow

UP ABOVE THEM, HIGH ON THE MOUNTAINSIDE, WAS ANOTHER MEADOW. THE GRASS LOOKED PLUSH AND GREEN. YOU COULD SEE THERE WAS PROBABLY LOTS OF CLOVER.

The Forest

The Hills

The River

The Low Meadow

Rocky and Blossom

ROCKY AND BLOSSOM CONSTANTLY
ASKED MURPHY IF THEY COULD
GO UP THE MOUNTAIN TO THE
HIGH MEADOW.

MURPHY WOULD
SHAKE HIS HEAD.

MURPHY KNEW A FEW THINGS
ABOUT ROCKY AND BLOSSOM.

THEY HAD BEEN
KNOWN TO MAKE
SOME BAD DECISIONS
OVER THE YEARS.

MURPHY ALSO KNEW THERE WERE **DANGERS** ON THE MOUNTAIN. IT WASN'T A GOOD PLACE FOR TWO SHEEP BY THEMSELVES.

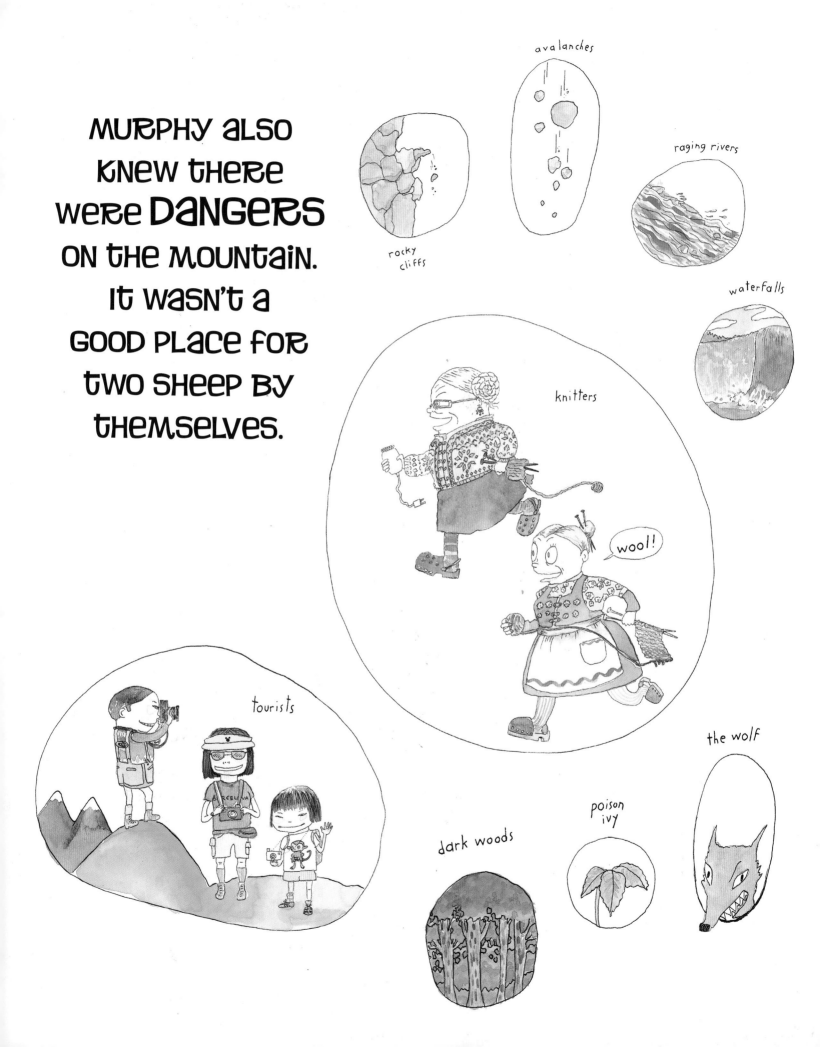

BUT BLOSSOM AND ROCKY COULD NOT STOP THINKING ABOUT THE OTHER MEADOW.

SO THEY WAITED AND WATCHED.

ONE DAY WHEN MURPHY WENT TO GET A DRINK OF WATER FROM THE STREAM...

...OFF THEY WENT!

THEY RAN AND RAN.

"Let's hide behind that rock!" said Blossom.

HE TOOK THEM HOME.

ROCKY AND BLOSSOM STILL
COULDN'T STOP THINKING
ABOUT THE HIGH MEADOW.

THEY BEGAN TO SNEAK AWAY
EVERY SINGLE DAY.

THEY WERE INCREDIBLY SNEAKY...

...BUT MURPHY WAS INCREDIBLY GOOD at FINDING THEM.

ONE MORNING MURPHY HAD TO HELP A LAMB GET HIS FOOT OUT OF A GOPHER HOLE.

BLOSSOM AND ROCKY MADE THEIR GETAWAY! (AGAIN.)

THE FOREST WAS DARK AND OVERGROWN.
THE TWO SNEAKY SHEEP RAN FOR A LONG TIME.

AFTER A WHILE, THEY STOPPED
BY A HUGE PINE TREE.

THEY walked around its large trunk.

AND RAN into the WOLF!!

HELLO.

ROCKY AND BLOSSOM WERE EXTREMELY STARTLED, TO SAY THE LEAST.

BLOSSOM AND ROCKY
BACKED AWAY SLOWLY.

THEN THEY TURNED
QUICKLY TO RUN.

BUT THE WOLF WAS BEHIND THEM!

THE SHEEP REALIZED
THEY WERE ON THE EDGE
OF A STEEP CLIFF.

THEY WERE IN **BIG** TROUBLE. (AGAIN.)

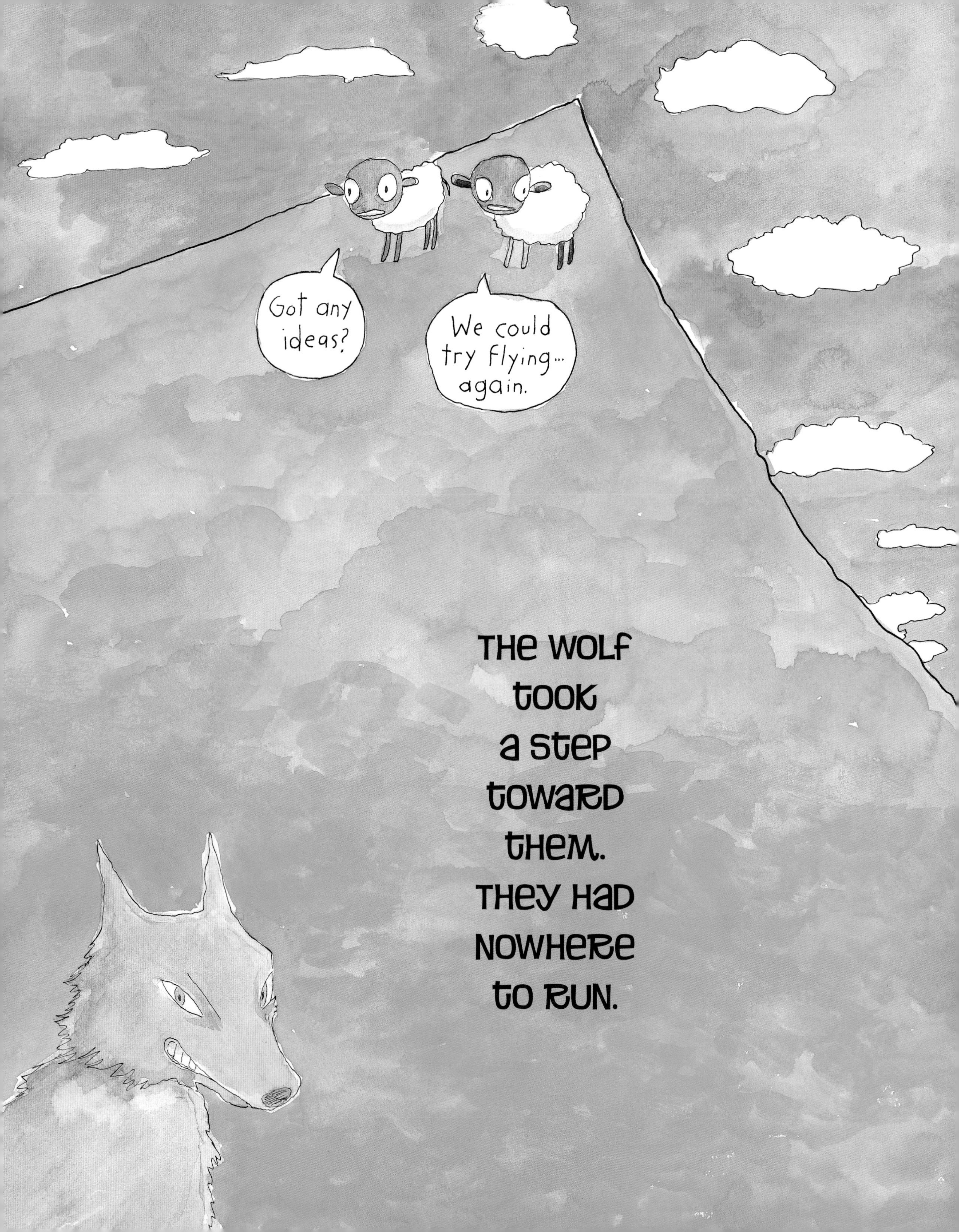

THE WOLF took a step toward them. They had nowhere to run.

SUDDENLY, MURPHY CAME FROM OUT
OF NOWHERE AND KNOCKED THE WOLF
DOWN THE CRAGGY EMBANKMENT!!

"RUN!" HE BARKED,

AND ROCKY AND BLOSSOM
DID JUST THAT.

THEY RAN AND RAN AS FAST AS THEY COULD BACK TO THEIR MEADOW. MURPHY FOLLOWED CLOSE BEHIND.

THE WOLF WAS GONE.

He's gone.

ONCE AGAIN, MURPHY TOLD THEM:

And you need to stay in the meadow!

AND that is what they DiD!